FIRST BUT FORGOTTEN

— THE UNTOLD STORY OF —

BRIDGET MASON

A FREEDWOMAN BECOMES AN ENTREPRENEUR

BY DR. ARTIKA R. TYNER

Consultant:
Dr. Dennis C. Dickerson
Reverend James Lawson Chair in History
Vanderbilt University

CAPSTONE PRESS
a capstone imprint

Published by Capstone Press, an imprint of Capstone
1710 Roe Crest Drive, North Mankato, Minnesota 56003
capstonepub.com

Copyright © 2025 by Capstone. All rights reserved. No part of this publication may be reproduced in whole or in part, or stored in a retrieval system, or transmitted in any form or by any means, electronic, mechanical, photocopying, recording, or otherwise, without written permission of the publisher.

Library of Congress Cataloging-in-Publication Data is available on the Library of Congress website.

ISBN: 9781669070115 (hardcover)
ISBN: 9781669070061 (paperback)
ISBN: 9781669070078 (ebook PDF)

Summary: You may have heard about Dred Scott's case to gain his freedom from enslavement. But just a year before the Supreme Court decision in Scott's case, Bridget "Biddy" Mason won her freedom in a California court—and then went on to become the wealthiest Black woman in Los Angeles. Uncover Mason's story of gaining her freedom, becoming an entrepreneur, and serving her community.

Editorial Credits
Editor: Ericka Smith; Designer: Sarah Bennett; Media Researcher: Svetlana Zhurkin; Production Specialist: Katy LaVigne

Image Credits
Alamy: FLHC DBM2, cover, North Wind Picture Archives, 7, 12, 18; Getty Images: Hulton Archive, 13, Los Angeles Times/Irfan Khan, 29, WireImage/Earl Gibson III, 25; Granger: ullstein bild, 11; Library of Congress: 19; Los Angeles Public Library: Los Angeles Public Library Legacy Collection, 15, Security Pacific National Bank Collection, 21, 23, 27; The New York Public Library: Schomburg Center for Research in Black Culture/Manuscripts, Archives and Rare Books Division, 24, Schomburg Center for Research in Black Culture/Photographs and Prints Division, 5; Shutterstock: Everett Collection, 9, 10, Julia Khimich (background), cover (right) and throughout, Nadegda Rozova (background), cover (left) and throughout; University of Southern California Libraries and California Historical Society: 17

Any additional websites and resources referenced in this book are not maintained, authorized, or sponsored by Capstone. All product and company names are trademarks™ or registered® trademarks of their respective holders.

Printed and bound in the USA. 5853

TABLE OF CONTENTS

INTRODUCTION
Los Angeles Historymaker 4

CHAPTER ONE
Enslaved Across the Country 6

CHAPTER TWO
Winning Her Freedom in Court 14

CHAPTER THREE
Real Estate Entrepreneur.................... 20

CHAPTER FOUR
Serving the Community 24

CHAPTER FIVE
Mason's Legacy............................ 28

Glossary 30

Read More 31

Internet Sites 31

Index............................... 32

About the Author 32

Words in **bold** are in the glossary.

INTRODUCTION

LOS ANGELES HISTORYMAKER

Bridget "Biddy" Mason was born into slavery. But a move to California—a free state—changed that. In 1851, her enslaver took her to the golden state. Before they could move out of California, free Black people Mason knew helped her gain freedom. Her case went before the court, and she was **emancipated**.

Once free, Mason worked as a midwife. She invested her pay in real estate. She became the first Black woman to purchase land in Los Angeles. Soon, she became one of the wealthiest people in the city. She was also a community leader.

Many people have heard of Dred Scott, who **petitioned** the courts for his freedom in 1846. Mason, however, is not as well known. This is her story.

CHAPTER ONE

ENSLAVED ACROSS THE COUNTRY

Mason was born on August 15, 1818, in Hancock County, Georgia. She was born enslaved. At a young age, she was taken from her mother. She was sold several times. Mason was enslaved on plantations in Georgia, Mississippi, and South Carolina. During most of her early years, she was enslaved on a plantation owned by John Smithson.

Mason was raised by older Black women. They taught her many skills. They taught her how to understand plants and their healing power. They also taught her how to deliver babies as a **midwife**.

An older enslaved woman taking care of young enslaved children

FACT Black midwives played an important role during slavery since they were highly skilled in providing medical care. Some were allowed to travel to other plantations and care for the sick. Others earned wages for their services.

In 1836, Mason was given to Smithson's cousin Robert Marion Smith and his wife, Rebecca, as a wedding present. Mason worked in the fields on their plantation in Mississippi. She also served as a midwife and a nurse. She helped keep everyone healthy. She took care of Rebecca, who was often ill. Mason also delivered Rebecca's six children.

Mason had a family of her own too. She had three daughters—Ellen (born in 1838), Ann (born in 1844), and Harriet (born in 1848).

A plantation on the Mississippi River in the 1800s

Mormon settlers traveling to Utah

Smith converted to Mormonism. The church asked members to come live in one central location— what would later become Salt Lake City, Utah. The Mormons wanted to build a community there. Smith answered the call.

In March 1848, Smith led his family and the people he enslaved to Utah. It was a journey of more than 1,700 miles (2,735 kilometers). Mason and her children were a part of this group.

After three years in Utah, Smith decided to move again. This time he was headed to California. There he would build a Mormon colony and start a cattle ranch. In 1851, he led the group to San Bernardino, California.

A Mormon settlement in California in the early 1800s

FACT During the 1840s, California had become known for the promise of wealth and riches. The land was fertile ground for farming—and gold.

But slavery was illegal in California. As they traveled west, Mason met free Black people. They encouraged her to **sue** for her freedom once she arrived there. One free Black couple, Charles H. and Elizabeth Flake Rowan, told her to take action right away.

But Mason did not try to gain her freedom immediately. She was enslaved in California for five years. While there, she met many free Black people. They also encouraged her to fight for her freedom.

Over time, Smith became worried that Mason and other enslaved people would seek their freedom. He decided to move to Texas. Texas was a slaveholding state.

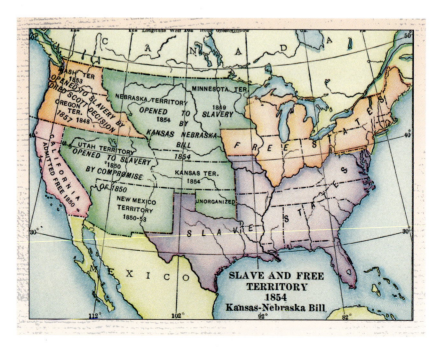

California as a Free State

In the mid-1800s, newly formed states in the West had a choice to make about whether they would allow slavery. California joined the Union in 1850 as a free state. But there were both free and enslaved Black people in California because the state did not actively enforce its ban on slavery. Slavery supported the economy. Enslaved people labored on the farms, worked in the gold mines, and helped to build up the land.

A Black miner in California in 1852

CHAPTER TWO

WINNING HER FREEDOM IN COURT

In 1855, Smith began preparing for the move. He decided to leave by New Year's Day of 1856.

But by the time Smith was ready to go, Mason's daughter Ellen was in a relationship with a free Black man, Charles Owens. When Owens heard that Smith was leaving for Texas, he took action. Owens wanted to protect Ellen and her family.

The Owens family brought a sheriff and a petition for a lawsuit to Smith's home. They claimed Smith was holding the Mason family unlawfully. The sheriff took Mason and her children into **protective custody**.

San Bernardino, California, around 1852, where Smith illegally held Mason and her family captive

A judge named Benjamin Hayes heard Mason's case. During the trial, Smith said Mason and her family were not enslaved. He claimed that they were his family. He said they wanted to move to Texas with him.

Mason's attorney did not show up for the trial. And it was illegal for Mason to testify. California law prevented a Black person from testifying against a white person in court.

But Judge Hayes found a solution. He called her into his **chambers**. He allowed her to share her story. She told him that she was enslaved by Smith.

Benjamin Hayes

On January 21, 1856, Judge Hayes freed Mason. He also freed 13 other people. After five years of being enslaved in California, Mason was ready to start a new life.

Mason's case was a great victory—but an unusual one. Different state and federal laws and practices made it difficult for enslaved people to gain their freedom through the courts. Free states did not actively enforce their laws. And the 1850 Fugitive Slave Act made things more complicated. It required enslaved people to be returned to their slaveholders even if they were in a free state.

Still, enslaved people across the nation fought for their freedom. Some brought their cases to court. Others escaped slavery through the **Underground Railroad**.

A formerly enslaved man captured and taken from his home in a free state in the 1850s

The Dred Scott Case

Dred Scott was an enslaved man whose enslaver brought him from Missouri, a slave state, to a free state (Illinois) and a free territory (Wisconsin). After returning to Missouri, Scott sued for his freedom in 1846. He claimed he should be free because he had entered a free territory.

Dred Scott

Scott's case made it all the way to the U.S. Supreme Court. In 1857, the Supreme Court ruled in *Scott v. Sandford* that enslaved Black people were property, not citizens, so Scott did not have the right to sue.

This case happened about a year after Mason's victory. It proved the courts were not always a good way to gain one's freedom. Slavery would have to be abolished through the highest law of the land—the U.S. Constitution—to ensure freedom for Black people across the country.

CHAPTER THREE

REAL ESTATE ENTREPRENEUR

Mason eventually moved to Los Angeles. She worked as an assistant, a midwife, and a nurse with Dr. John Strother Griffin. She helped deliver hundreds of babies.

Mason earned $2.50 per day. She saved her wages. On November 28, 1866, Mason purchased a piece of land. She used $250 to buy two lots of land on Spring Street—now part of downtown Los Angeles. She became one of the first Black women to buy land in the city. Over time, the area became a **bustling** area with new homes and businesses.

Spring Street in Los Angeles in the late 1800s

At first, Mason used the land for gardening. She later built homes on the land and rented them out. She also started a daycare center.

Eventually, Mason bought more land and sold it for a profit. She bought land on Olive Street for $375. She later sold it for $2,800.

Mason also sold part of her land on Spring Street for $1,500. On the remaining land, she constructed a building. She rented the bottom level to businesses. She and her family lived on the upper floor.

By the late 1880s, Mason had built a business worth $300,000. That sum would have been about $10 million in 2023. She was the wealthiest Black woman in Los Angeles.

Olive Street in Los Angeles around 1887

CHAPTER FOUR

SERVING THE COMMUNITY

Mason was also committed to serving her community in Los Angeles. She helped the poor, the sick, and the imprisoned. She built a traveler's aid center, an elementary school, and an orphanage.

In 1872, Mason became one of the founders of First African Methodist Episcopal Church. It is the oldest Black church in Los Angeles. The church's first services took place in her living room. As of 2023, the church had more than 19,000 members. It still serves as a key resource in the community.

FACT The African Methodist Episcopal (AME) Church was founded in 1816 by Bishop Richard Allen in Philadelphia, Pennsylvania.

Bishop Richard Allen

First African Methodist Episcopal Church
in Los Angeles in 2012

In 1884, there was a flood in Mason's community. Many people were injured. Others lost their homes and their jobs. Mason helped take care of her neighbors. She asked a local grocer to provide food to people in need and covered the expenses.

Mason taught her family to serve their community too. Her grandson Robert Curry Owens followed her example. He invested in real estate and became one of the wealthiest Black men in Los Angeles. He donated money to organizations that supported the Black community like the Tuskegee Institute—now Tuskegee University—an educational institution in Alabama for Black people.

Damage from the 1884 flood in Los Angeles

CHAPTER FIVE

MASON'S LEGACY

Mason passed away in her home on January 15, 1891. But she continues to inspire others to serve their communities. She is known as the "Grandmother of Los Angeles" because of her community service.

Her descendants are following in her footsteps. They lead the Biddy Mason Foundation. The organization supports education and healthcare efforts for those in need.

Mason has also been recognized for shaping California's history. On March 27, 1988, the first Black mayor of Los Angeles, Tom Bradley—a member of First AME Church—laid a tombstone on her unmarked gravesite. On November 16, 1989, Biddy Mason Day was first celebrated. A Los Angeles park named Biddy Mason Memorial Park was created in her honor. And in 2022, Mason was inducted into the California Social Work Hall of Distinction.

Mason's life serves as an example that hard work and dedication can change your life. It can also create opportunities for others to have a brighter future.

Amanda Gorman, an American poet, at Biddy Mason Memorial Park on Mason's 200th birthday in 2018

FACT The Biddy Mason Memorial Park is located in downtown Los Angeles on Spring Street—where Mason's home once stood. It has a visual timeline of Mason's life. It begins with her fight for freedom and shows how she worked hard to become a successful real estate entrepreneur.

GLOSSARY

bustling (BUS-ling)—filled with activity

chamber (CHAYM-buhr)—a room

emancipate (ih-MAN-sih-payt)—to set free from the power and control of another person

midwife (MID-wahyf)—a person who assists women in childbirth

petition (puh-TISH-uhn)—to make a formal request

protective custody (pruh-TEK-tiv KUHS-tuh-dee)—placing someone under the watch of the police for their safety

sue (SOO)—to start a legal process to seek justice

Underground Railroad (UHN-dur-ground RAYL-rohd)—a series of safe houses and secret routes; many enslaved people freed themselves by traveling to the North from one house to another

READ MORE

Jones-Radgowski, Jehan. *Harriet Tubman*. North Mankato, MN: Capstone, 2020.

Tyner, Artika R. *The Untold Story of John P. Parker: Underground Railroad Conductor*. North Mankato, MN: Capstone, 2024.

White, Arisa and Laura Atkins. *Biddy Mason Speaks Up*. Berkeley, CA: Heyday, 2019.

INTERNET SITES

Britannica Kids: Biddy Mason
kids.britannica.com/kids/article/Biddy-Mason/633109

Britannica Kids: Slavery
kids.britannica.com/kids/article/slavery/353782

National Park Service: Bridget "Biddy" Mason
nps.gov/people/biddymason.htm

INDEX

African Methodist Episcopal Church, 24
Allen, Richard, 24

Biddy Mason Foundation, 28
Biddy Mason Memorial Park, 28, 29
Bradley, Tom, 28

California, 4, 11–13, 16, 18, 28

First African Methodist Episcopal Church, 24, 25

Georgia, 6
Gorman, Amanda, 29
Griffin, John Strother, 20

Hayes, Benjamin, 16–18

Illinois, 19

Los Angeles, California, 4, 20–23, 24–27, 28, 29

Mason, Ann, 8
Mason, Ellen, 8, 14
Mason, Harriet, 8
midwives, 4, 6, 7, 8, 20

Mississippi, 6, 8
Missouri, 19

Owens, Charles, 14
Owens, Robert Curry, 26

Rowan, Charles H., 12
Rowan, Elizabeth Flake, 12

Salt Lake City, Utah, 10
San Bernardino, California, 11, 15
Scott, Dred, 4, 19
Smith, Rebecca, 8
Smith, Robert Marion, 8, 10–12, 14–16
Smithson, John, 6, 8
South Carolina, 6

Texas, 12, 14, 16
Tuskegee University, 26

Underground Railroad, 18
U.S. Supreme Court, 19
Utah, 10–11

Wisconsin, 19

ABOUT THE AUTHOR

Dr. Artika R. Tyner is a passionate educator, award-winning author, civil rights attorney, sought-after speaker, and advocate for justice. She lives in Saint Paul, Minnesota, and is the founder of the Planting People Growing Justice Leadership Institute.